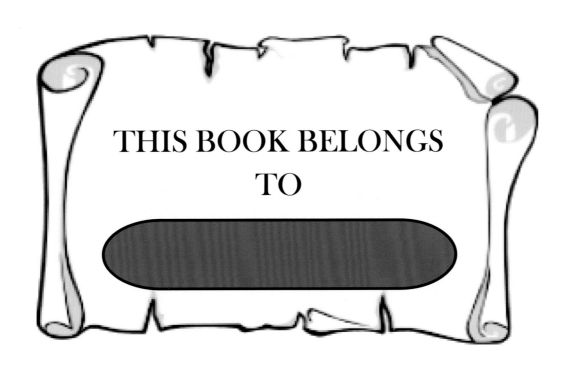

THIS BOOK BELONGS TO

Hi Lovelies!

Today I'll be taking you on a journey to NA NA LAND!

On this adventure, we'll learn a little about the *Chronicles of NANIE*

YES! You are right!

This is a book about me.

By the end of the journey you would have gotten to know me a little better, and maybe we can be FRIENDS!!!

It all began in **1989**.

I was born in Brooklyn, NEW YORK on the day everything begins to

Blossom, March 21st… **SPRING!**

Mom and Dad thought I was going to be a Boy, but Ta-da!

Surprise! Surprise!

It's a GIRL!!!

My First **GIFT** was my Name.

It was at Brookdale hospital that Dad gave me the name: **N A N I E**

My mom is also called **NANIE**. Kinda cool don't you think?

I've never met any other person who has the same name as me.

Do you know that each person's name is IMPORTANT?

Names are mostly chosen out of LOVE

And it can connect us to <u>People</u>, <u>Things</u> and <u>Places</u> around the World.

There's a STORY to each name.

OH!

Have you ever wondered what your Name means?

I asked my mom about the meaning of my name, **NANIE**

She said that it means, "**SWEET PERSON**".

Thinking about this makes me SMILE.

Where did my name come from?

My name originates from the KPELLE language.

The Kpelle language is spoken by the Kpelle tribe in LIBERIA.

That's my mom's homeland.

Mom says that my name is pronounced different from how it is spelt.

Although it is written as **N A N I E**, it is pronounced, **NEH—NU.**

(It's funny cause no one pronounces it that way.)

West Africa

GUESS WHAT!

My name, **NANIE** also originates from two other languages:

FRENCH and HEBREW

Surprisingly my name has the same meaning in both languages:

NANIE = **GRACE** ✸ **FAVOUR** ✸

It is amazing how a name can have the <u>same</u>

OR

<u>different</u> meaning in various countries and languages.

Teachers and Students at school often spell my name in different ways.

I think it's because my name has many vowels in it.

N A N I E

It could also be because of the way I pronounce it to them.

My best guess is that it's because <u>few</u> people in America

have the name, **NANIE**.

Whenever my name is spelled correctly it brings Joy to my heart,

and a smile on my face.

WHO AM I?

The most common way people spell my name is, NANI.

In Arabic, NANI *means* — **CHARMING.**

In Hawaiian, NANI *means* — **BEAUTIFUL.**

In Hindu, NANI *means* — **Maternal GRANDMOTHER**

In Japanese, NANI *means* — **WHAT?**

In Swahili, NANI *means* — **WHO?**

I'M

INTERNATIONAL!

The name N A N I E is <u>not</u> my only name.

Nanie is my first name … (*little secret*)

I didn't know that my first name was/is <u>NANIE</u> until I turned 16 years old!

How could this be?

(*The story behind this mystery will be revealed in a later book; stay tuned!*)

Before age 16, I knew my name as, **CHIOMA**.

Everyone called me **CHIOMA**, I thought it was my first name.

This name was given to me in honor of my Father's eldest sister.

West Africa

CHIOMA means, **GOD is GOOD**.

The name originates from the IGBO language spoken in NIGERIA.

I Love the name **CHIOMA**; it's a powerful name.

Although I was born in New York, USA

I grew up in Port-Harcourt, NIGERIA. *(My father's homeland)*

While living in Nigeria, everyone called me by the name, **CHIOMA**

Unlike my first name, <u>Nanie</u>, **CHIOMA** is a popular name in Nigeria.

No one ever spelt my name wrong.

Everywhere I went; School, Church, or the Market place,

I could always find someone with the same name, **CHIOMA**.

It's pretty awesome!!!

In fact there are songs written about my name in Nigeria.

I believe it's because the meaning of the name is in honor of GOD.

The name **CHIOMA** makes me feel special.

I left Nigeria at age 16 to live with my mother in Washington, USA.

My mother began calling me by my very first name, **NANIE**.

From then on everyone called me, NANIE.

CHIOMA is my middle name, but sometimes it's like my first name.

Family and childhood friends in Nigeria still call me **CHIOMA**

I like that they do so; it reminds me of my life in Nigeria.

It's important that I embrace all of me, and be proud of my Family.

I ANSWER TO BOTH

My name is **NANIE CHIOMA MEMEH.**

I'm Nigerian, Liberian and American.

I take pride in my name, **ALL** of it.

It tells a story of <u>Love</u>, and <u>History</u> of my roots.

I'm glad I know my story; your name has a story too!

Names have **POWER.**

Take a look at the last page and think about your name.

You will be happy to know your story.

WHAT IS YOUR NAME?

Parent and Child Activity:

Write your Story

MY NAME IS: ----------------------------------

Who gave you your name? ---------------------------

Do you know the meaning of your name? ---------------

If yes, what is it? -----------------------------

Were you named after someone, place or thing? ------

If yes, who? Where? What? ------------------------

What is the origin of your name? -------------------

*** You can send your story to the Author: The.nanieshow@gmail.com

Special thanks to: Mommy Nanie Weah Weah (aka) Mabel Mucbah

Mommy Julie Egbuhuzo

Sister Noralee Green

FOLLOW ME

@NannerLandKids -

-NannerLandKids -

#MyNameIsNANIE